Mermaid KINGDOM

Mermaid Kingdom is published by Stone Arch Books
A Capstone Imprint
1710 Roe Crest Drive
North Mankato, Minnesota 56003
www.capstoneclassroom.com

Copyright © 2015 Stone Arch Books

All rights reserved. No part of this publication may be
reproduced in whole or in part, or stored in a retrieval
system, or transmitted in any form or by any means,
electronic, mechanical, photocopying, recording, or
otherwise, without written permission of the publisher.

Library of Congress Cataloging-in-Publication data is
available on the Library of Congress website.

ISBN: 978-1-4342-9693-1 (library binding)
ISBN: 978-1-4342-9697-9 (paperback)
ISBN: 978-1-4965-0187-5 (eBook PDF)

Summary: Since her dad died, Shyanna has not been
able to sing. But in one bold move, all of that is going to
change thanks to the mermaid Melody Pageant. Shyanna
must conquer her stage fright and other obstacles to
bring song back into her (and her mom's) life.

Designer: Alison Thiele

Artistic Elements: Shutterstock

Printed in Canada.
092014   008478FRS15

Shyanna's song
3
6jpb   06/20/16

Shyanna's Song

by Janet Gurtler

illustrated by Katie Wood

STONE ARCH BOOKS
a capstone imprint

Mermaid Life

⭐ Mermaid Kingdom refers to all the kingdoms in the sea, including Neptunia, Caspian, Hercules, Titania, and Nessland. Each kingdom has a king and queen who live in a castle. Merpeople live in caves.

⭐ Mermaids get their legs on their thirteenth birthdays at the stroke of midnight. It's a celebration when the mermaid makes her first voyage onto land. After their thirteenth birthdays, mermaids can go on land for short periods of time but must be very careful.

⭐ If a mermaid goes on land before her thirteenth birthday, she will get her legs early and never get her tail back. She will lose all memories of being a mermaid and will be human forever.

✫ Mermaids are able to stay on land with legs for no more than forty-eight hours. Any longer and they will not be able to get their tails back and will be human forever. They will lose all memories of being a mermaid.

✫ If they fall in love, merpeople and humans can marry and have babies (with special permission from the king and queen of their kingdom). Their babies are half-human and half-merperson. However, this love must be the strongest love possible in order for it to be approved by the king and queen.

✫ Half-human mermaids are able to go on land indefinitely and can change back to a mermaid anytime. However, they are not allowed to tell other humans about the mermaid world unless they have special permission from the king and queen.

Chapter One

I had a plan. And unlike some of my plans, this one was brilliant. I thought about it while I watched my best friend's purple tail sparkle and glitter as she swirled around Walrus Waterpark with her baby sister. Jewel was giggling with delight as Cora twirled around and around.

Cora didn't know how lucky she was. She often assured me that being a big sister was a lot of work and often annoying, but I still wanted to have a sister. Unfortunately, that wasn't really an option.

My dad disappeared two years ago. Neptunia may be the best kingdom in the ocean, but there are always dangers underwater. From humans and nets to sharks and storms, the ocean is a dangerous place to live. Anything could happen at any time, and nobody really knows what happened to my dad.

Cora glanced over. "Why do you look so sad, Shyanna?" she asked as she put Jewel down in the sandbox in the middle of the park.

"I'm not sad," I told Cora. It wasn't really a lie. Not completely. "I'm thinking." That part was definitely true. Thinking about my plan.

"Thinking?" Cora shook a finger at me. "You have that look!" Cora swam over to the swing set I was perched on and flipped around in figure eights in front of me.

"What look?" I batted my eyelashes and opened my eyes wider. Sometimes I practiced my expressions in front of a mirror, so they looked super authentic. It sounds weird, but it really does help.

"Your 'I'm about to get myself into trouble and drag Cora along in the current' look," she said. She grinned and tried to rock me off the swing. I held on tighter and laughed.

"No," I said. "I won't involve you. I promise."

"You say that every time! And every time, somehow, I'm right in the middle." Cora threw her head back and laughed. "Good thing I love you." The sound of her laugh was so enchanting that a school of curious catfish swam over to see what was happening. Cora waved them away and then swooped back to her sister, scooping her up in her arms. Jewel giggled and stared up at Cora, adoration shining in her sea-blue eyes.

"So," Cora said to me. "What is the plan?"

"I want to win the twelve-year-old age category in the Melody Pageant," I blurted out. "I mean," I corrected myself and spoke softer and slower, "I'm hoping to be selected for the finals. I know that winning isn't everything."

Everyone in the kingdom goes to the Melody Pageant. It is the biggest and oldest celebration in Neptunia. It takes place in the courtyard in Neptunia's majestic castle, where the King and Queen live. The best part of the celebration is the talent competition during the pageant. It is simply magical. And winning wasn't really my main objective, but it's always hard to rein in my competitive side.

"I entered my name yesterday!"

"You did?" Cora slid onto the bench across from me, rocking Jewel in her arms.

Every year the King and Queen select the finalists from a special conch shell. Any mermaid could enter, but I never had the nerve to try — until now. Until now, I was too scared.

But ever since my dad disappeared, my mom had been miserable. She used to swim around singing all the time. And she had the most magical voice ever! We all loved to hear her sing, especially my dad. But now she wouldn't even hum, let alone sing. I needed to bring music back to my mom. She was ready, and so was I.

Cora frowned. "You're a beautiful singer, Shy, but isn't there one problem?" she asked. "A problem with a capital *P*?"

"Stage fright," we both said at the same time.

I sighed deeply. "Maybe we could enter the duet contest. You could sing with me?" I suggested. "I'm not as nervous when I sing with other people."

Cora laughed. "I'm the worst singer in Neptunia."

"You are not!" I said.

"I prefer sports," Cora said. "But I'll do what I can to help. Like when you helped me train for the Dolphin swim meet."

Cora put the *best* in best friend. We smiled at each other, remembering the fun we'd had getting her ready for the competition. I'd worn a timer around my neck for weeks and encouraged her as she swam faster and faster. I'd cheered extra loud when a gold medal was draped around her neck.

"With your help, I can do it. I know I can," I said with confidence.

"But why?" she asked. "Why now?"

Unable to contain myself, I leaped up and swam in a circle.

"If I make it to the finals, my mom will have to come to the Melody Pageant and enjoy music again," I said.

"You really think she would go?" Cora asked.

"Yes," I replied.

"But your mom stopped singing in your cave," Cora said as she rocked her sleeping sister. Her point popped my happiness bubble.

Ever since my dad disappeared, my mom refused to go to the Melody Pageant. She wouldn't even listen to music anymore.

She believed my dad was captured in a fishing net because humans heard him singing. He'd been out in the ocean, past Neptunia, to try to find a special shell for their anniversary. He could never resist singing when he was out hunting for treasure, which was his very favorite thing to do.

"She doesn't sing because it makes her sad. But if she goes to the pageant, she'll remember that it can make her happy too! She'll see how wonderful it is!" I refused to feel guilty. It was for my mom's own good. And mine too. We needed more happiness in our cave. I wanted to be able to sing songs that reminded me of my dad.

"Did she say she wants to go?" Cora asked.

I plunked down on the bench again. "No. But I feel it. It's sort of like when she makes me eat krill medicine. I don't want to do it at the time, but it makes me feel better after."

Cora frowned.

"There is one other problem, Shyanna." Cora tapped a finger against her cheek. Her eyebrows were still pressed into a disapproving line. I already knew what she was going to say, but I still asked.

"What?" I asked.

"Your competitive spirit will take over, and you won't be happy unless you win."

I put both hands on my hips and frowned. "It won't be like that."

"Remember when you entered that sand building contest and you stayed up all night and built the biggest sand castle in the kingdom?"

"Well, I won, didn't I?" I reminded her.

"Yes, but you didn't sleep for forty-eight hours! And that time you entered the clam-eating contest?"

I bit my lip. I had refused to give up until I won, but I was sick for days afterward. Okay, so maybe I did like to win. But didn't everyone?

"Well, I have the perfect song. I just need help getting the pitch right." I frowned. "Don't you think I have a chance to win the twelve-year-old category?"

Cora reached for my hand and squeezed. "Of course you have a chance," she said. Then she pulled back. "But that's not supposed to be the point. You want to show your mom how great singing is and how happy it can make you. You want to be able to sing at home and maybe conquer your stage fright while you're at it. Right?"

"I know. This is about my mom. And remembering my dad. I promise." I closed my eyes, imagining myself singing on the stage in front of the King and Queen. I pictured a winner's crown being placed on my head.

"Shyanna?" Cora said sharply, snapping me back to reality.

I coughed and then swallowed, ignoring a tickle at the back of my throat. Instead I smiled at Cora to show her my plan wouldn't get her in any trouble at all.

"Don't worry," I said. "My plan will work. It will help my mom get her sparkle back and remind her of the positive powers of music and how much my dad loved it."

And if I happened to win my age category . . . well, how bad would that be?

Chapter Two

Boom! Bang! Bang!

Cora and I both turned when we heard the sudden noises outside of Walrus Waterpark.

"They're starting to set up!" I said.

The selection ceremony was later that day, and there was a flurry of activity. Mermen swam by, carrying colorful flags and tables. A group of mermaids followed carrying colorful sea glass jewels and huge flower decorations.

"What time does the selection ceremony begin?" Cora asked.

"At dusk." It was only a few hours away.

"Let's take Jewel home," Cora said. "We have work to do. We'll go to your cave so that I can comb out your hair and shine up your tail," Cora got up from the bench and began to swim.

I clapped my hands. Cora would make me look extra pretty.

"What seashell top are you going to wear?" she asked as I hurried along behind her. "Something green?" she said before I could answer.

"Yes! Green!" I agreed excitedly.

"The green will contrast nicely with the golden flecks in your tail. I'll rub your tail with fish oil to make it extra rainbow-like."

Like most mermaids, my tail was a mix of colors. Cora's spectacular single-shade purple tail was the envy of all of Neptunia. I'd always wanted a single-shade tail, but Cora always said she wished for a tail more like mine.

We swam past the pink coral pillars of the Queen's court tower. It was adorned with precious pearls of the sea, the official jewel for all of the mermaid kingdoms. Merpeople lit the entrance to the castle and the courtyard with jellyfish; others were hanging puffer fish lanterns in the tower above the courtyard. The majestic castle looked even more magical than normal.

It was all so exciting. I couldn't stop grinning at everyone bustling around. Everyone was happy and festive. I wanted my mom to feel some of the joy!

"Come on, Cora," I said. "We have a lot to do before the big ceremony."

"I'm coming," she said with a smile.

We swam to Cora's cave first. As the oldest sibling and the official family babysitter, Cora had to fight off the rest of her three younger sisters, all of them chattering and wanting her attention. She tucked Baby Jewel into her crib, and then Cora announced to her family that I had put my name in the conch shell. Her whole family cheered and promised to cross their fingers for me.

Her mom gave her permission to help me get ready, so Cora changed into a fancy purple shell top and off we went. She arranged to meet her family in the courtyard later to watch the selection ceremony.

Mom was still working at the Fish Factory when we got to my cave. Cora and I hurried to my room, and she got to work, helping me beautify. She combed my hair until it was free of tangles and shiny, and then she put it up in beautiful shell clips. She glossed my lips and shined my tail with special oils.

"You look beautiful, but what are you girls doing?" came a voice from my doorway. I glanced over and saw that Mom was watching us. She must have gotten home early.

"Today's the selection ceremony for the Melody Pageant," I announced, as if she didn't know and hadn't been trying to avoid it.

"I know, but . . ." she trailed off, puzzled by the primping that was going on in my room.

"I put my name in the shell," I explained.

"Oh, Shyanna," she said. She blinked, and tears filled her eyes. I was afraid she was going to cry, but then she smiled, and I realized her tears were tears of joy. "I'm very proud of you."

"You are? Really? You're not mad?" I asked.

"Of course not. You love to sing. I know that. Just like your dad. And if you're willing to take on your stage fright . . . well, that's brave and amazing."

"I really want to sing in the Melody Pageant, Mom." I held my breath as she bowed her head for a moment. I bit my lip and avoided looking at her, or I might start to cry. I didn't want to make my mom sad or upset.

"You really want a chance to sing in the pageant, Shyanna?" She took a deep breath and then let it out.

I nodded. "More than a crab loves to crawl."

"Then I hope the King draws your name," she said with pride in her voice.

"Thank you," I said. "Will you come to the selection ceremony?"

"I can't," she said. "But I promise if your name is called, I will come to the pageant. Deal?"

"Yes!" I yelled as I gave her a huge hug.

Everyone told me I got my beautiful singing voice from my mom. She told me I got her nervousness too. It was so sad that she wouldn't sing anymore. I was sure she only needed a little push to find joy in singing again. Going to the pageant would be the push she needed.

Chapter Three

The King was the most handsome merman in Neptunia, with long blond hair that flowed under his golden crown. The beautiful Queen, on the throne beside him, shimmered in the jellyfish light. The King and Queen wore dazzling purple robes made from the dye of sea snails.

The Queen looked radiant as she held up one of the conch shells filled with contestants' names. The King announced the last eleven-year-old finalist in his booming voice. The Queen put down that conch shell and picked up the conch shell with twelve-year-old names inside. This was it!

I could barely breathe as I listened to the first names being read. There were only ten spots, and they were filling up.

"Our second to last twelve-year-old is . . ."

"Rachel Marlin," the King announced.

My tail deflated. A beautiful mermaid with curly red hair swam up front. I didn't recognize her, which was weird since I knew everyone in Neptunia.

"Who's that?" I whispered, but Cora was busy with Jewel and didn't look up.

Finally the Queen held out the conch shell again.

"And the last name for the twelve-year-old competition is . . ." the King said and paused for effect. He cleared his throat.

I crossed my fingers as the seconds ticked by. Even Jewel stopped crying. Cora glanced up at the King and then at me. What was taking so long?

"Shelby Stewart."

My insides crumbled. I swallowed a lump that sprang up in my throat. I wouldn't get my chance to sing in the pageant. I wouldn't win. Worse, my mom wouldn't come to the pageant.

There was clapping, and then a pause as a mermaid with a pink and turquoise tail swam forward. She didn't swim to sit with the other finalists; instead, she swam to the Queen and whispered in her ear. The Queen nodded, gave her a hug, and then whispered something to the King.

"The last contestant is unable to compete, so I will draw again for our final competitor." The King held up a piece of paper. "The final competitor in the twelve-year-old category is . . . Shyanna Angler."

My ears roared louder than big waves crashing to shore. Cora hugged me and screamed, and I managed to swim up front. Cora and her family cheered my name extra loud.

I was in shock! I couldn't believe the King had drawn my name out of the shell! I knew it had nothing to do with skill, as it was just luck if you got chosen. But I didn't care! This was a huge moment for me!

* * *

"Mom!" I yelled when I swam back into our cave. "Mom!"

She was waiting for me in the front room. I swam into her arms, and she hugged me tight. "Cora's mom called and told me you were picked. I'm so proud of you," she said.

I let out the breath I'd been holding. "You're really not mad?"

"Of course not. It's what you wanted. You need to go after what you want. I know I've been strict about the singing," she said. "But maybe it's time to bring some joy back into our house."

"I couldn't agree more," I said with a smile. "So you're really going to come to the pageant? I don't want to sing without you there."

She hugged me again, even tighter. "Of course I'll be there," she promised. "And you must practice."

I took a deep breath. I hated to ask, but a part of me wanted to not only compete, but to win. "Do you think you could help me? I think I can deal with the stage fright, and I have my song picked, but I can't get the pitch right. Everyone says you're the best soprano singer in the kingdom."

"Oh, Shyanna," she said and swam over to the sandbag chair across the room. "I can't sing anymore. I just can't. Not since your dad . . ." She plopped down on the chair and fiddled with her tail.

I nodded and tried not to show my complete disappointment. It wasn't fair of me to even ask. She had agreed to come, and she was even encouraging me to sing again. I shouldn't push for more, even though I wanted to.

She glanced up. "I heard the Queen hired a new singing instructor. He just moved to Neptunia from Caspian. He has a daughter about your age, actually."

Caspian was the kingdom closest to the mainland. Rumor had it that some merpeople from that kingdom had met actual humans! I'd always wanted to see a human. I wondered if the singing instructor or his daughter had ever met humans.

"I'll ask if he can give you lessons," my mom said. "Your dad would have wanted that."

"Oh, thank you, Mom. Thank you!" I told her. Hearing her mention my dad again was a good sign.

"After all," she continued. "The worst he can say is no."

Chapter Four

Nothing could wipe the smile off my face as
Mom and I headed to meet the new music instructor.
Along the way, merpeople waved at me and called
out congratulations for being selected to sing at
the pageant. Being treated like a celebrity was fun!
Imagine if I actually won the pageant!

A flurry of nerves started in my stomach. I would
be singing on a stage in front of everyone, which
was really scary. But I had my mom's secret to help
fight off stage fright. I would be fine. I just had to be

confident. If I could master the song, I might even win. I just had to focus.

Cora's voice echoed in my head. "Remember. It's not about winning. You get to face your fear, and you get your mom to come to the pageant."

"Hello!" a voice called as we swam past the cave of my mom's friend, Pearl Sparkles. "So good to see you out and about!" She swam out to greet us, and the two of them started to chatter.

It was obvious my plan was already working. Mom was out of the cave and talking to her oldest friend, all because of the pageant! I twirled around in the water waiting for them to finish up, and soon I got bored. I signaled to my mom that I was going on ahead, and she nodded her permission.

I swam all the way toward the last caves at the edge of Neptunia. The voice instructor lived in a new neighborhood for the King and Queen's special helpers. Their row of caves was larger than ours, but they seemed vacant because hardly anyone lived there yet. No merpeople played in the yards or worked outside. I swam closer to the caves we were headed for, and then a sound reached me and crept into my soul.

Singing. Only it was so beautiful and haunting that I almost started to cry. The high notes melted my heart, and the low notes flowed behind them and softened my soul. The voice drifted up and down and lingered and floated, almost as if it were a living part of the water. It was the most amazing thing I'd ever heard. Even more beautiful than the most beautiful whale songs.

Mesmerized, I swam toward the sound and peered into the cave it came from. A mermaid sat on a rock, facing away from me. She had beautiful curly red hair hanging down her back. As she reached the end of the song, she turned her head. Her eyes were closed, but I recognized her profile. Oh no! It was her. The girl from the pageant. The new twelve-year-old mermaid! I swam away quickly, before she could

open her eyes and see me. I didn't want her to think I was spying on her. Her voice was so beautiful, and I knew then that I had no chance to win against her. I wanted to get away from that voice!

I hurried back through the neighborhood toward Pearl's house, but Mom met me about halfway back. "Are you okay, Shyanna?" she asked. "You look as if you've seen a ghost fish!"

"Fine," I lied. "I'm fine." I hadn't seen a ghost fish. I'd seen my pageant crown being pulled off my head. I know I kept telling myself that winning didn't matter, but it did!

Mom frowned at me but pulled me along, leading the way back to the new neighborhood. "There's the cave." She pointed at the cave where the redhead had been singing and swam on ahead toward it.

The redhead must be the instructor's daughter! No! I couldn't meet her. I couldn't. I didn't want her to know I needed help when she was already so amazing.

"Actually," I told my mom quickly, "I'm not feeling well." I treaded water and refused to follow her any farther. "And I changed my mind. I don't think I need lessons after all. I can learn the pitch myself."

She swam back to my side and smiled. "Pre-stage fright? It's okay. Don't be nervous. Come on, Shy. It's his job. He'll help you."

She took my hand and pulled me beside her until we were in front of the cave. I was so flustered that I didn't know what to do. She rang the bell, and the beautiful mermaid swam to the opening. She looked at both of us and smiled brightly. "Hello!"

"Hello! We're looking for Seth Marlin," my mom told her.

"You're Shyanna, right? From selections? It's going to be so fun! I've never sung in public before. It's all so exciting!" The girl stopped talking for a minute and turned and yelled for her dad.

She turned back to me. "I'm Rachel. His daughter." She smiled and held out her hand.

I squinted as my mom shook the hand of the girl who was going to snatch my crown from me. "Nice to meet you," my mom said. "This is Shyanna's first time singing in front of a crowd too. We heard your dad was an excellent coach. We're hoping he'll help her get her pitch just right."

I didn't say anything. I didn't want this girl to hear me sing. She'd laugh at my awful pitch. She'd know how much better she was.

"Would you like to come in and wait? I think he's on the phone talking with the Queen about her voice lessons."

"Thank you," my mom said.

"No," I said at the same time. I held my stomach. "Sick," I said. I coughed for effect. "We should go."

Rachel looked at me and moved back a tiny bit. My mom frowned. I pulled on her arm. "We should go. Now."

"Don't you want to talk to my dad first?" Rachel asked. "I'm sure he'd love to help you."

My cheeks were as red as lobster tails. "It's okay," I said again. "I'm not feeling well. And I'm not sure if I need a coach after all. Bye."

I swam away, not giving my mom any option but to follow. I heard her tell Rachel to apologize to her dad for us, and then she swam up beside me. I swam faster.

"Shyanna." She grabbed my tail, so I had to stop. Then she put her hand on my forehead. "You're not warm. Are you sure it isn't nerves?"

"Maybe," I said and tried to swim away.

She held my tail. "I know you're nervous, but you can't waste Mr. Marlin's time like that. It's very rude. We should go back and apologize."

"No," I cried. "I'm not going back!"

And then the sound coated the water around us — the beauty of Rachel's singing. I put my hands over my ears and shook my head, trying to keep the sound out. I knew I was acting like a baby, but I didn't care.

"Shyanna." My mom looked toward the cave and then back at me. "Is that Rachel?"

I nodded and dropped my hands from my head. "She's going to be in the pageant," I said. "And she's twelve, and she's the best singer I've ever heard in my life." I sighed.

"That doesn't matter," my mom said. "You have a beautiful voice too."

"Listen to her," I said. "She's amazing. I can't let her hear me try to reach notes I might not even be able to reach. It's embarrassing. She's obviously going to win. I shouldn't even try."

Mom crossed her arms and stuck out her lips. "Is that the reason you're suddenly feeling sick?"

I nodded and tried not to cry.

"Oh, Shyanna," she said. "You put your name in the shell and were selected. You can't back out now."

"But that —"

"Shyanna!" Mom said as she cut me off. "I'm proud of you for even trying. For facing your fears.

It's not always about winning. Your dad would want you to sing. He would be so proud."

She put her arm around me. "Come on," she said. "Let's go home."

She was right. I was so happy that we were talking about my dad again, and it made me happy to see her happier too. But Cora was also right. I really wanted to win the pageant. Why couldn't I make my mom happy and also be the big winner? I just had to think of a way to beat Rachel.

Chapter Five

The next day my throat was sore. Maybe my bad sportsmanship was actually making me sick. I gargled with sea-salt water, and that seemed to help for a while. Afterward I sang arpeggios in my room and tried the song I picked. I still couldn't get the right pitch. I needed that pitch to have any chance of beating Rachel. I thought about picking a different song, but this was my dad's favorite song. I knew it would be extra special to my mom, so there was no going back.

I sang and sang until my voice was almost gone, and then I glanced at my clock and groaned. Oh no! I was late! I was supposed to meet Cora at Walrus Waterpark ten minutes ago. I rushed out of my cave without even brushing my tangled hair.

I hurried toward Walrus Waterpark but slowed down when I got close. Cora was twirling in circles in front of the swings, which wasn't unusual since she is always moving. What made me stop and hesitate was the mermaid perched on the swing.

She had a big smile on her face, and her gorgeous hair was flowing behind her as she moved. It was Rachel. Even worse, little Jewel sat on her lap and was smiling up at her. Jewel would never swing with me. And she rarely even smiled at me. This mermaid was really starting to annoy me.

I turned around, about to swim away and go home, but Cora shouted my name. "Shyanna! You're late! Come meet Rachel. She's coming to our school next month! She'll be in our class!"

I bit my lip to stop myself from saying something mean and remembered that Cora had been distracted when Rachel's name was selected from the conch shell. Cora obviously didn't know that Rachel was my biggest competition. Plus, we didn't need another friend. We had each other.

"Great," I said. I tried to smile, but my lips wouldn't cooperate. "We've met." I floated in front of the swing set, unwilling to sit beside her. "She's singing in the pageant too," I told Cora. "In the twelve-year-old category."

"How cool! Now I have two people to cheer for," Cora said. She clearly didn't see how annoyed I was. Why was she being so nice to someone she didn't even know?

"Hi, Shyanna. Are you feeling better?" Rachel asked. She looked so genuinely concerned that I felt a little guilty about how rude I was being. In fact, I think the guilt was making me feel sick, as my throat was aching. It even hurt to swallow.

"I told my dad you stopped by," she went on. "He said he'd love to help you with your song."

"No. It's okay. I decided I don't need help." My cheeks burned. Cora was looking at me with confusion, but after hearing Rachel sing, I didn't want her dad's help. I couldn't let her know my weaknesses.

"Wah!" Jewel started to shriek, and I smiled down at her. I wanted to give her a high five, but Cora plucked her off Rachel's lap and swam in circles, trying to distract her.

"Do you want to practice together?" Rachel asked. "I love duets."

"Hey, maybe you could sing a duet with Rachel!" Cora said to me. "That would help with your —"

"NO!" I shouted before Cora could reveal to Rachel that I had stage fright.

Rachel blinked. Her smile went a little wobbly. I thought about her being new to Neptunia. She'd had to leave behind all her friends at Caspian. Then again, once everyone heard her sing, she'd have lots of new friends here. More than me, probably.

"Shyanna?" Cora said, staring at me like I'd lost my mermaid mind.

I looked away. "I mean maybe," I said. "But if you sing a duet, you can't win the category trophy."

"I thought you didn't want to win," Cora said and stopped twirling. Jewel screeched unhappily.

"I don't," I lied. "I just want to sing alone."

Cora gave me a dirty look and then tickled Jewel until she giggled.

"Swing with me?" Rachel said to me while Cora was distracted. I knew Rachel was just trying to be nice, but it was hard to be nice back. Before Rachel moved here, I was the front-runner to win the pageant. Now I barely had a chance. She was so talented and sweet it was hard to stomach it.

I reluctantly slid onto the swing beside her. I started pumping my tail hard to get up higher and higher on my swing so I wouldn't have to talk to her.

But Rachel smiled and started swinging harder too. "So," she said, "how's the school here? Are the mermaids nice?"

I bit my lip and thought about what to say. "Pretty nice." I glanced around Walrus Waterpark, avoiding her eyes. "I mean. There are lots of unspoken rules you might not know. Being new and all."

"Really? Like what?" She started swishing her tail, but lightly, so the swing only moved a little.

"Well . . ." I said and let my voice drag off.

"What?" she asked.

"Well. Since you are new here, the merkids might be kind of jealous if you win the Melody Pageant." I took one hand off the swing and tried to comb it through my messy hair.

"Really?"

"Well, I don't know for sure, but it wouldn't be great. The pageant is such a big deal."

"I know." Rachel sighed and glanced over to where Cora and Jewel were playing in the water box. "My best friend, Owen, doesn't care about the pageant," she said sadly.

"Your best friend is a boy?"

"Um . . . sort of," she said with a sad smile.

"Cool." I picked a strand of seaweed from my hair and thought about how hard it must be to leave behind your best friend.

"I don't want to win the pageant if the other merkids won't like me. Maybe I should forfeit?" she asked.

I fidgeted on the swing and cleared my throat.

"I was so nervous to enter," she said. "And now that I'm picked, I think I should go through with it."

"I only entered so my mom would have to come to the pageant. She doesn't usually go," I said.

"Really? Me too! I mean for my dad. Even though he's a singing instructor and he totally should, he hasn't been to the pageant for a few years. I was hoping to get selected so he'd have to come and see me," she said.

"Huh." I couldn't believe we actually had something in common. Our swings were moving in sync, and I glanced sideways to see her face. "Why hasn't he gone?"

Rachel stopped pumping her tail, and her swing slowed down. She lowered her eyes and looked sad. "My mom was killed by sharks a few years ago. It happened when we were traveling to the pageant. Bad memories, I guess."

I stopped pumping my tail. "I'm sorry," I said. My heart hurt for her. I could completely relate.

"Yeah. She wasn't that great of a swimmer," she says. "It was awful."

I blinked. It must have been awful. Now I felt extra bad about being so weird and mean. And I lied to her about other merkids being jealous of her. I was the only one who would be jealous.

"Hey," said Cora, who was floating toward us. "You two want to come to my house? I have to get Jewel home. She's cranky, and she needs a nap."

"Sure!" I said and jumped off the swing.

"I should get home." Rachel slid off her swing. "To help out my dad. But thanks for asking."

"You sure? We'd love if you could come." Cora narrowed her eyes at me.

"I'm sure. See you both around." Rachel waved and then darted away.

"See you soon!" Cora called after her and then turned to me, narrowing her eyes even more.

"She's competing in the Melody Pageant?" she asked as we started swimming toward her cave. Jewel hung onto her around her neck.

I nodded, trying to avoid her gaze.

"And I bet she's really good." She stopped swimming so fast I bumped into her. "I heard what you told her about the merkids not liking her if she wins the pageant. Why did you tell her that, Shy?"

My cheeks turned bright red. "Well, she'll be new. The merkids might be jealous." My voice sounded weak and unsure even to me.

"Are you sure it's not you who's jealous?" Cora asked. Jewel screeched, so Cora started swimming again. Jewel needed a nap, but it sounded like she was judging me too.

I felt my eyes tearing up. "Her voice was the most amazing voice I'd ever heard from anyone in Neptunia, and not just the twelve-year-olds."

"So?" Cora asked and stopped swimming again, patting her little sister on the back to calm her.

"I want to win." I stared down at my fins.

Cora placed her free hand on her hip. "I thought you wanted to conquer your stage fright and help your mom get singing and happiness back in her life. Why is winning so important to you?"

"Winning is important to everyone!" I said.

"If you want to win so badly, you should want to compete against the best singers," she said. "Plus, winners don't cheat and lie."

"I didn't cheat," I whispered, but I don't think she heard me.

"I'm going to go home alone," she told me. "Jewel needs a long nap."

And then she swam off, swishing her glorious purple tail behind her.

What had I done? Had I just lost my best friend over my own jealousy?

Chapter Six

My hands were shaking when I got home from the waterpark, and I was crying like a baby. Now my stomach and my throat hurt! What if Cora never wanted to talk to me again? What would I do without my best friend? I went to my room, picked up my phone, and called Cora, but there was no answer.

Cora had probably already asked Rachel to be her new best friend. Rachel was nice. And she was from Caspian. She'd probably seen humans, and she'd even had a boy for a best friend. She was much more of a merry mermaid than I was. And once everyone heard her amazing voice, she'd be the most popular mermaid at school. There wasn't much I could do about it now.

Suddenly tired, I lay down on my bed, staring at posters of my favorite bands hanging on my walls. They were gifts from Cora for my twelfth birthday. It made me start crying all over again.

* * *

"Shyanna?"

My mom's voice startled me, and I gasped. I didn't even realize I'd fallen asleep, and for a moment, I couldn't tell if it was morning or night.

"You've been sleeping?" My mom swam over and put her hand on my forehead. "You're warm," she said. "Are you feeling okay?"

The memory of everything rushed back. "I'm all right," I croaked. I didn't want to worry her. In fact, that would just make everything even worse.

"Are you nervous about the Melody Pageant?" she asked.

"No," I said quickly.

She watched me for a moment. "You're sure?"

I fake smiled and nodded.

"Come on, then. I made crab legs." I followed her to the kitchen, sat at the table, and tried to eat, but it hurt my throat to swallow.

After a while, I gave up. "I guess I'm not very hungry," I told her and pushed the plate away.

"What's wrong?" Her brow furrowed in concern.

A tear slid out of my eye. "I had a fight with Cora," I said instead of telling her about my sore throat. If I told her my throat hurt, she would pull me out of the pageant, and all this would be for nothing!

"Oh dear. What was the fight about?" She patted my head and then cleared our plates from the table.

I shrugged, not wanting to tell her what I'd done.

"I'll clean up. You get to bed. Things will look better in the morning. You and Cora will make up."

She swam over and hugged me tight and then shooed me off to bed.

I went back to my room, but before I lay down, I picked up my phone to call Cora one more time. She didn't pick up. With a heavy heart I tucked myself under the covers on my bed, and exhausted, fell fast asleep. All night long, I dreamed about being trapped by humans and living all alone in a giant fish bowl.

* * *

When I woke up in the morning, my head was pounding. Swallowing hurt. Breathing hurt. This was not good.

"Hello?" I said to my pet snail, Speedy, to try out my voice. It worked but sounded a little off. After going to the kitchen to gargle with seawater, I tried to sing. Ultra relieved to hear my singing voice work, I opened wider to hit a high note.

That's when it happened. A horrible crack. It sounded like a seal barking.

I tried again. Worse.

Sighing, I wrinkled up my nose, got out the dreaded krill medicine from the top cupboard, and swallowed back a whole tablespoon. I attempted the high note again.

Seal bark. This was serious.

Panicking, I hurried to the bookshelf and took out the *Magic Mermaid's Book of Cures* that all mermaids received when a merbaby was born. The *Magic Mermaid's Book of Cures* is only to be used in emergencies. Mermaid magic is not something the King and Queen encourage us to fool around with. They limit the use of magic, because their job is to keep merpeople safe. All merpeople know that magic has risks and shouldn't be used for fun.

I flipped to the symptom page and pinpointed the problem. Laryngitis. There was a cure, but the picture and description made my heart skip a few beats. A crushed red dwarf mussel shell would cure the throat infection, but they were only found on

Platypus Island. The island was outside of Caspian, which was close to land. Merkids couldn't leave Neptunia alone until they turned thirteen, and I was only twelve. And even when we turn thirteen, it's not safe to go so close to land.

I tried calling Cora one last time, not sure if I wanted her to come with me or talk me out of it, but she didn't pick up. That settled it. I had to go on my own. Laryngitis couldn't stop me from getting my mom to the Melody Pageant. I needed that cure. It might be dangerous, and not very smart, but what other choice did I have?

Chapter Seven

No one even paid attention as I swam past the gates that marked the entrance to Neptunia. With the Melody Pageant coming up, merpeople were too busy to notice me. I swam on and on past kingdoms I'd only visited briefly with my parents.

It was lonely and kind of scary until a whale and a group of dolphins swam up beside me. It's hard to be afraid or sad when swimming with a whale and dolphins. We all swam farther and farther until we finally reached Caspian. It was as beautiful as I'd

heard and almost as big as Neptunia. On the far side of Caspian were the gates to enter Platypus Island, and a big problem for me.

Sharp-eyed Octopi guarded the gates, but I had an idea. Distraction.

I told my dolphin friends the plan, and they whistled and clicked their approval. The whale watched from his side eye and frowned. I patted his belly, letting him know I'd be all right.

"I have to get a special shell," I told him, "to cure my voice."

The dolphins darted ahead. My whale friend couldn't come any farther because the passage narrowed, and his oversized body wouldn't fit through.

Then the dolphins got to work. They jumped and swirled and dragged their bellies on the bottom of the sea, whipping up an instant underwater sandstorm. It gave me enough time and camouflage to swim past the guards.

It was instantly darker once I entered Platypus Island, and fear bubbled under my fins. I glanced around nervously and tried to remember where the red dwarf mussel shells were located. I'd memorized the map that was in the *Magic Mermaid's Book of Cures*. I just had to stay calm and focus.

I swam and swam but couldn't find the shells. Then I noticed that the tide was beginning to go out. I had to find the shells and get home. I swam close to the shore and began to search. I looked and looked. The water was getting shallower. It frightened me, but I couldn't leave until I found the shells.

Suddenly, a red shimmer caught my eye. It was a red dwarf mussel shell! I dove deep, but a wave lapped over me, and the shell disappeared under the sand. Sighing, I forced myself to slow down so I would not disturb the water, and soon I saw it again — another flash of red!

I dove down fast, and my fingers grabbed at it. The sand drifted around, but I held on. The shell was mine! I had the cure! I'd be able to sing in the Melody Pageant. If I could convince Rachel not to sing, I might even win! I kicked my tail hard to swim away, but a piercing pain stopped me.

"Ouch!" I yelled. My fin was wedged underneath a rock. I wiggled around, trying to pull my tail out without dropping the shell. But the movement just made it worse. The pain was terrible!

The water continued to recede with the tide, and then my tail was only covered in a thin layer of the salt water my gills needed to keep my tail intact. The tide was going out quickly, and with each wave, less and less of the shore was underwater. I was going to get stuck on land if the water kept receding. This was not good. Not good at all.

If I got stuck on land now, I'd get human legs early, and my mermaid tail would never grow back. I would be stuck on land forever! I would never be able to return to Neptunia, and I wouldn't be able to call myself a mermaid ever again! And as soon as my tail was gone, my mermaid memories would be gone as well. I wouldn't remember ever being a mermaid.

My mermaid life would totally disappear.

My panic increased as the water got lower and lower. Pulling didn't help, and I started crying. I didn't want to be alone, stuck on land forever, never able to get my tail back. I wanted to stay a mermaid.

The water lapped out farther. My crying got louder and louder.

"Hello?" called a sweet voice from the shoreline above the rocks. "Are you all right down there?"

I clapped my free hand over my mouth. It was a human! Was I going to end up like my dad — lost and never to return undersea again?

Chapter Eight

"I'm coming down to help," the voice called. It was definitely a human voice.

Oh no! I couldn't let myself be seen by a human! Humans and merpeople do not mix. If I talked to a human before my thirteenth birthday, I would lose my tail forever. I would have legs for the rest of my life!

All of these rules about humans and merpeople interacting were to protect Mermaid Kingdom and all the merpeople. Only in special circumstances were merpeople and humans allowed to mix (and only with the magic protection of the King and Queen), and even I didn't fully understand what those circumstances were. All I knew was that if a human saw me, I would lose my tail and be stuck on land forever with no mermaid memories.

I was pretty much out of options. Either I was stuck on land and would get my legs too early (forgetting my entire mermaid life and becoming a human forever), or a human would talk to me and I would get my legs too early (forgetting my entire mermaid life and becoming a human forever).

The human jumped down to the rocks. She was getting closer and closer. I closed my eyes, as if it that would make anything better. Maybe if I couldn't see the human, she wouldn't bother me? I just didn't know what else to do.

"Shyanna?" the human called. "Are you stuck?"

How did this human know my name? I wondered. I opened my eyes. It was Rachel!

Rachel was a human?

"Rachel?" I gasped. "But your tail . . . you have legs." I started crying as she bent down and pulled at the rocks to release my tail. "What are you doing? You're only twelve. You'll never get your tail back!"

Had I done this to her? Made her go to shore too early? Was it all my fault? I didn't like her very much, but that didn't mean I wanted to ruin her entire life!

She ignored me and focused on freeing my tail. She pulled so hard it hurt more than sea urchin stings, but I was free!

"Swim, Shyanna, swim," she said. "You need to swim now."

I was too shocked to move. Rachel had rescued me, but she'd never be a mermaid again. Then Rachel dove into the water, and a fin flapped, splashing my face. Her tail had reappeared. I stared at it and then up at her face.

She swam on, tugging me behind her, pulling so hard that the shell I was holding fell out of my hand. I screamed, but Rachel dove deep and came up holding out her hand. The red dwarf mussel shell was inside.

She put the shell in my hand. "I hope it was worth all this trouble." Rachel swam slowly, but I grabbed her with my free hand.

"Did you lie about your age?" I asked. "Are you already thirteen?"

"I'm twelve." Rachel rolled her eyes in annoyance. "What were you doing so close to land? You could have been seen by humans."

"But you had . . . legs . . ." was all I could manage. "Your tail . . ."

Rachel sighed and rolled her eyes again, but at least she started talking. "My mom was human before she became a mermaid, which is why she couldn't swim as fast as the other mermaids. My dad fell in love with her when he spent time on shore. Because their love was so strong, she was given special permission from the Queen to become a mermaid and marry him. That makes me half-human. I can go on land whenever I want. For as long as I want."

"You can?" My mouth wouldn't close. "That is . . . so . . ." I tried to think of the word.

"Freakish?" she said and glared at me.

"Cool," I told her. "That is so cool."

She tilted her head. "Really? You don't think I'm a freak?"

"How could I think you are a freak? I think you're amazing," I said. "You saved my life!"

"What were you doing alone outside Neptunia, anyway?" she asked.

I glanced at the shell in my hand. "Something is wrong with my throat. I can't sing very well, and I needed a cure." And then something occurred to me. "Wait a minute. What were *you* doing outside Neptunia all alone?"

"I was visiting Owen. I heard you crying as I was leaving. And lucky for you I did!"

"You were with your best friend from Caspian?" I asked.

"Owen is a human," she said casually, and then she somersaulted.

Human? Rachel was so glamorous. Wait until Cora found out! But then I remembered. Cora wasn't talking to me.

"Rachel?" I called. Her eyes were wide, her mouth wider. She looked frozen. A shiver ran down my tail. I turned my head.

Sharks! And they were heading right for us.

Chapter Nine

The sharks advanced slowly as though they were taunting us. They grinned to show off rows of pointed teeth. My heart pounded. My eyes almost bulged out of my head. I fumbled and reached for Rachel's arm. "Swim. Come on, Rachel! Swim!"

She didn't move. "Shortfin Mako," she whispered without blinking. "The fastest shark in the ocean. They killed my mom." The sharks kept moving closer, not even bothering to chase us yet.

Rachel started to cry.

"No!" I said. We wouldn't go down like this. Eaten by sharks. I needed to sing in the Melody Pageant to make my mom happy again. Plus, I really didn't want to die yet.

Then I remembered the bedtime story my mom read to me over and over when I was small. The story was about mermaids with voices so powerful they could stun sharks into submission. I glanced down at my dwarf shell, crushed it in my hand, and tossed it in my mouth. Then I began to hum the song I was planning to sing in the pageant.

"Sing," I told Rachel, but she was so terrified she didn't move or take her eyes off the sharks.

"Mermaid music, hear us now," I sang. The sharks didn't stop. I cleared my throat as the last of the crushed shells dissolved.

"Mermaid magic, show us how." My voice rang clearer. My pitch was perfect!

The sharks stopped. Rachel glanced at me. I nodded, encouraging her to join me. She had to know the song. It was a mermaid classic. The sharks started moving toward us again. I sang louder.

"Mermaids sing together and free."

Rachel smiled. The song finally seemed to break her from her spell. She reached for my hand and sang the next chorus with me.

"The music we make rules the sea." Our two voices blended together, powerful and perfect. We lifted our chins and belted out the next verse.

The sharks stopped, and their eyes glazed over and rolled back. They looked like they'd gone to sleep. "It's working," I whispered. "Keep singing."

We sang another verse, and the sharks didn't move. "Go, go, go!" I whispered. Rachel and I kept holding hands, and I swam faster than I had ever swum before. Cora would have been proud. We raced back into Neptunia and into safety.

Once we were inside the kingdom, I finally stopped, bending over. I was out of breath but completely exhilarated.

Rachel threw her arms around me, and we hugged and laughed with relief.

"Thank you," Rachel said. "You saved my life. I was so scared. I couldn't think or move."

"I guess we're even now," I told her.

She stopped smiling. "Even," she agreed. And then she took a deep breath. "But I need to ask you for a favor."

I nodded. After that near-death experience, I felt almost as close to her as I did to Cora.

"Anything," I told her. "What favor?"

She bit her lip and glanced around, but the sea creatures around us weren't paying us any attention.

"Don't tell anyone," she whispered, refusing to look at me. "Please."

"You mean about . . ." I pointed down to her tail.

She finally looked at me, still biting her lip and looking nervous.

"Sure, if that's what you want. But why? It's so cool!" I said.

"Some merpeople don't understand. Everyone at Caspian knew, and I didn't have friends. I used to go to shore a lot. That's how I met Owen."

It was obvious that the other mermaids were just jealous of her, which was exactly how I had felt as well. Rachel was fabulous. And she could use legs whenever she wanted! I felt so bad for the way I had acted toward her.

"That won't happen here," I told her. "I'll make sure of it." I rushed forward and hugged her tight, ashamed of myself for being mean to her before.

"Everyone is going to love you. Especially when you win the Melody Pageant."

Her face brightened, but she shook her head. "I thought you said it was a bad idea to enter."

"No," I admitted. "The truth is, if you sing, you'll win for sure, and everyone from school will be excited. They'll want to be your friend!"

"You really think so? That's not what you said before," Rachel said.

"I know, and I'm sorry. I was really jealous of you," I said.

Before Rachel could answer, we heard someone yelling for us.

"Oh my goodness, there you two are," a voice called loudly.

We both looked ahead. Cora swam toward us. "I've been looking everywhere for you two. Your parents are worried. They're out together now, searching the other kingdoms. What have you been up to?"

Rachel and I exchanged a look. I nodded. I'd keep the secret for now. "Are you still mad at me?" I asked Cora instead of answering her question.

Cora crossed her arms and narrowed her eyes.

"I told Rachel the truth," I said quickly. "That if she sings in the pageant, all the girls will fight to be her friend."

"Then I'm not mad anymore. Not at all." Cora rushed forward and hugged us both. "I was really worried about both of you. Thank goodness you're both safe!"

"Let's get back," Cora said. "You have to get ready to sing in the pageant."

That's right, I thought. *All of this, and I still have to perform in public.* It made me more nervous than I had been when I left Neptunia alone.

Chapter Ten

The morning of the Melody Pageant, my mom helped comb my hair until it was as smooth as polished sea glass. She placed the flower and shell headpiece Cora had made on my head. My mom had even bought me a new top. It sparkled and shined and made me feel like a princess.

Once my mom finished helping me get ready, Cora and I swam over to Rachel's cave to do our final primping together. It was so fun! Every once in a while, Rachel's dad popped in and out of her room to make sure we were all doing okay. He was such a good dad.

"Do you want help with your song?" he asked. "You never did ask me to coach you."

"I'm okay," I told him. "But thank you." The mussel shell seemed to have solved my voice problems. My notes were strong, and my pitch was even. All I needed to do was conquer my nerves.

Just then my mom showed up. Mr. Marlin and my mom had agreed to get to the pageant early to save us good seats. It was such a relief to see my mom excited about singing again and going out with a new friend. On top of that, she was smiling!

"We'll take you girls out for a celebration after the show, no matter who wins," Mr. Marlin said.

"Rachel's going to win," I said.

"Shyanna's going to win," Rachel said at the same time.

We looked at each other and giggled.

"It doesn't matter who wins," my mom said.

"Just go out there, and sing your hearts out! And don't forget to have fun."

It warmed my heart to hear her say that. Maybe someday she'd start singing again too!

Finally, when it was time to go, Cora, Rachel, and I swam side by side toward the courtyard. My heart felt like it was going to burst open like a frost flower on ice. The day would be filled with music, food, friends, and happiness.

We swam into the courtyard. It looked even more amazing than it had the day of the selections. The stage was lit up with glowing jellyfish. Sea flowers in full bloom lined the seats in the audience. Everything was bright and colorful. Shells and jewels sparkled on the thrones of the King and Queen.

Suddenly, a curtain came down in front of the stage, and the jellyfish dimmed their lights. The curtains flew open, and the pageant began with a beautiful group song from last year's winners. The water vibrated with the sound, and then the pageant was underway. I clapped and mouthed along with contestants, and then before I knew it, the King was calling the twelve-year-old finalists to the stage.

I was so nervous I couldn't get up. I didn't move until Rachel grabbed my hand and pulled me with her to the seats on the side of the stage where contestants waited for their turn to perform. It felt like I was dreaming. This didn't feel real at all.

But just a few minutes later, the King announced my name. "Next up is Shyanna Angler! Let's hear it for Shyanna!"

The piano player began playing my song. I stared out at the audience. Rachel elbowed me in the side. I didn't move. The pianist paused and then replayed the introduction to my song. I didn't move.

"Shyanna," Rachel whispered. "It's your turn. Go! Sing for your mom!"

Some people in the audience started to mumble. The King and Queen stared at me. My face burned. I was too terrified to move.

I closed my eyes and tried to remember what my mom had told me. She'd told me to imagine that all of the mermaids were her. It should have helped. It should have relaxed me.

But it didn't. I couldn't move.

And then fingers gently brushed my shoulder. I opened my eyes. Cora floated in front of me, holding out her hand. "Come on," she whispered. "I'll sing it with you. You can do this, Shyanna."

I shook my head. Cora kept tugging, and Rachel looked back and forth at us. She floated up from her seat, gave Cora the thumbs-up signal, and then swam to my other side. They each took one of my hands.

"Shyanna Angler and I have decided to perform as a group instead of solo," Rachel announced to the audience. "Along with our friend, Cora Bass."

"No," I hissed to Rachel. "If you sing with me, you'll forfeit your chance to win our category."

We'd both be disqualified from the twelve-year-old category.

"Never mind," Rachel said through her teeth, smiling. She gestured toward the confused-looking pianist. The Queen clapped her hands and nodded her approval. The pianist started the song from the beginning one more time.

Rachel began to sing. She sounded amazing. Cora opened her mouth and sang along in a lower range. She smiled the special smile of a true best friend, and with the two of them encouraging me, I was pulled out of my stupor. And then, as if we'd rehearsed it a million times, we sang and harmonized the rest of the song. It sounded incredible!

When we finished, the entire crowd went crazy. Merpeople clapped their hands and floated up into a standing ovation. It was amazing! Even the King and Queen looked impressed.

I gazed into the audience, my heart filled with happiness and love, and spotted my mom. She was smiling, bursting with pride. Her face glowed. She looked happier than I could have hoped.

Finally the King waved his hands to quiet the audience. "A spectacular performance," he announced, "but not eligible for the twelve-year-old category."

I looked at Rachel to see if she was disappointed, but she smiled.

"That was the best! It doesn't matter that we can't win," she said.

"It really doesn't," I agreed. And surprisingly, that was the truth. I knew we'd be best friends for life, and that was the biggest win of all.

The King called for the next contestant, and as we swam back to our seats, Cora swam in close. "I knew somehow you'd drag me into your plan," she whispered to me and laughed.

It was the best Melody Pageant I'd ever been to, and maybe, just maybe, the best day of my life so far. There would be singing in our cave from now on!

Legend of Mermaids

These creatures of the sea have many secrets. Although people have believed in mermaids for centuries, nobody has ever proven their existence. People all over the world are attracted to the mysterious mermaids.

The earliest mermaid story dates back to around 1000 BC in an Assyrian legend. A goddess loved a human man but killed him accidentally. She fled to the water in shame. She tried to change into a fish, but the water would not let her hide her true nature. She lived the rest of her days as half-woman, half-fish.

Later, the ancient Greeks whispered tales of fishy women called sirens. These beautiful but deadly beings lured sailors to their graves. Many sailors feared or respected mermaids because of their association with doom.

Note: This text was taken from The Girl's Guide to Mermaids: Everything Alluring about These Mythical Beauties *by Sheri A. Johnson (Capstone Press, 2012). For more mermaid facts, be sure to check this book out!*

Talk It Out

1. To help her mom, Shyanna had to face her stage fright. Talk about a time when you faced your fears.

2. Shyanna lied to Rachel to improve her chance of winning the pageant. If you overheard Shyanna, what would you have said? Would you have told Rachel or not said anything?

3. Did you have any idea that Rachel had a secret life on land? Why or why not?

4. Would you want to be a mermaid? Why or why not?

Write It Down

1. When Shyanna heard Rachel sing for the first time, she was jealous. Write about a time when you were jealous and how you handled it.

2. Shyanna and Rachel ended up helping each other when they needed it most. Write about a time when you helped a friend.

3. Pretend you are a reporter and write a newspaper article about the Melody Pageant. Be sure to include details about the decorations, fashion, and the talent show.

4. Were you surprised by the ending of the book? Write a paragraph supporting your answer.

About the Author

Janet Gurtler has written numerous well-received YA books. Mermaid Kingdom is her debut series for younger readers. She lives in Calgary, Alberta, near the Canadian Rockies, with her husband, son, and a chubby Chihuahua named Bruce. Gurtler does not live in an igloo or play hockey, but she does love maple syrup and says "eh" a lot.

About the Illustrator

Katie Wood fell in love with drawing
when she was very small. Since graduating
from Loughborough University School of
Art and Design in 2004, she has been living
her dream working as a freelance illustrator.
From her studio in Leicester, England, she
creates bright and lively illustrations for
books and magazines all over the world.